The Halfway Party

Story by Pauline Cartwright

Illustrations by Rachel Tonkin

Contents

Rigby

HOUGHTON MIFFLIN HARCOURT
Supplemental Publishers

www.Rigby.com
800-531-5015

Chapter 1

The Great Idea

"I'm not going to be here for your birthday,"
Gus told Adam.
"Our family is going away for the weekend."

"Oh, no!" said Adam.
"And I won't be here for yours.
Dad has to go into the city that day,
and we are going with him."

The boys always went to each other's birthdays.
Gus's birthday came first,
and Adam's was two weeks later.

All day, Gus thought about
how he and Adam would miss
each other's birthdays.

Suddenly, he had a great idea!
"I know what we can do about our birthdays,"
Gus whispered to Adam.

Mrs. Nelson looked over at the boys.
"Please stop talking," she said to them,
"and finish your work. The bell is about to ring."

After school, Gus told Adam his great idea.

"We don't have to miss
each other's birthdays," he said.
"We could have one party instead of two."

6

"You're right," said Adam.
"Let's have it on the weekend
between our birthdays."

"Yes!" said Gus, laughing.
"We can have a halfway party!"

Chapter 2

Where Will We Have the Party?

The boys' parents thought that a halfway party
was a great idea, too.
"Now you just have to decide where to have it,"
said Gus's mother, smiling.

"We could have a picnic party
on our farm," said Gus.

"We have a new grill in our backyard,"
said Adam. "We could use that.
My dad's really good at cooking hot dogs."

"If it's a halfway party," said Gus,
"we should have it somewhere halfway!"

"You're right again," Adam said, laughing.

Gus drew a large map of the two farms
in the dust on the ground.

Adam pointed to a spot on the map.
"That valley goes through both farms.
It would be a good place to have the party,"
he said.

"We could have it under the trees
by the stream," said Gus.
"But let's hope it doesn't rain
because that stream fills up with water
very quickly."

Chapter 3

A Loud Rumbling Sound

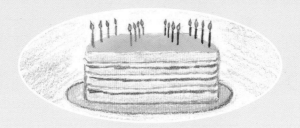

On the morning of the party,
Gus jumped out of bed early.
He was very excited.

His father was already out on the farm,
and his mother was making
a huge birthday cake.

"This year you can have one cake—half each,"
she said, smiling.
"There will be enough room
for both sets of candles."

Suddenly, there was a loud rumbling sound
in the distance.

"That sounds like thunder," said Gus's mother,
going over to the window.
"Oh, dear," she said.
"Those dark clouds could mean
that it will rain soon.
We do need rain on the farm."

"Not today, though," Gus said with a groan.

All day, Gus and Adam kept watching
the clouds and hoping that it wouldn't rain.

They didn't want to have their party
in one of the barns.

But later that afternoon, the clouds rolled away
and the sky was clear again.
Everyone arrived with food and presents,
and the games began.

"This is the best party ever!"
Adam shouted to Gus
as they sped down the grassy hill
on pieces of old cardboard.

"Let's have a halfway party every year!"
Gus shouted back.